LEE & LOW BOOKS Inc., 95 Madison Avenue, New York, NY 10016
leeandlow.com
Book design by David and Susan Neuhaus/NeuStudio. Book production by The Kids at Our House.
The text is set in 14/24-point Hank. The illustrations are hand drawn and digitally colored.

Manufactured in Malaysia by Tien Wah Press, March 2014
10 9 8 7 6 5 4 3 2 1
First Edition

Library of Congress Cataloging-in-Publication Data
Godin, Thelma Lynne.
The hula-hoopin' queen / by Thelma Lynne Godin ; illustrated by Vanessa Brantley-Newton. — First edition.
pages cm
Summary: Kameeka yearns to continue her hula-hooping competition with her rival, Jamara, rather than help prepare for
Miz Adeline's birthday party, and "the itch" almost ruins the party before the girls learn who the real winner is.
ISBN 978-1-60060-846-9 (hardcover : alk. paper)
[1. Competition (Psychology)—Fiction. 2. Birthdays—Fiction. 3. Parties—Fiction. 4. Responsibility—Fiction. 5. African
Americans—Fiction. 6. Harlem (New York, N.Y.)—Fiction.] I. Newton, Vanessa, illustrator. II. Title. III. Title: Hula-hooping queen.
PZ7.G54372Hul 2013   [E]—dc23   2013015548

The Hula-Hoopin' Queen

by Thelma Lynne Godin

illustrated by

Vanessa Brantley-Newton

Lee & Low Books Inc.
New York

To Pat, the best Hula-Hoop maker.
You make my world go round. —T.L.G.

For Zoe, Ben, and Chyna,
my Hula-Hoopin' family —V.B.-N.

Today is the day I'm going to beat Jamara Johnson at hooping. Then I'll be THE HULA-HOOPIN' QUEEN OF 139th STREET! Jamara says she's gonna be the queen forever, but last week I almost beat her.

I sort through my hoops and pick out my favorite. And then I feel it comin' on. The itch. The Hula-Hoopin' itch. My fingers start snappin', and my feet start tappin'. My hips start swingin', and I'm just reachin' for a hoop when Mama says . . .

"Girl, don't you even think about it. You know today is Miz Adeline's birthday."

Heat washes up over me, and I stamp my foot. Don't get me wrong. I love Miz Adeline. She lives right next door. Miz Adeline took care of Mama when she was little, and she took care of me too. She's like my very own grandmama.

"But, Mama," I burst out. "I can't help with Miz Adeline's party. I'm supposed to meet Jamara. Today's the day . . ."

Mama stands as still as water in a puddle. She gives me her look. Then she hands me a broom.

I sigh loudly and start sweeping. But when Mama's not watching, I push my favorite hoop a little closer to the door with my toe.

Mama and I dust every room and scrub down the floors. We polish each window 'til we can see clear to New Jersey.

After that I peel potatoes while Mama starts mixing up her special double-fudge chocolate cake.

"Kameeka, set the oven to 350 degrees," Mama says as she empties the
last of the sugar into the mixing bowl. "And add sugar to the grocery list."
I push the button on the oven and look out the window. It's already
getting late. I bet Jamara's telling everyone I'm too scared to hoop her.

While the cake bakes, we make up plates of fancy sandwiches. Then Mama slices strawberries and shows me how to make whipped cream. When the timer rings, Mama opens the oven.

"Kameeka!" Mama yells as she checks the oven temperature. "You only set it to 250 degrees!"

Miz Adeline's birthday cake looks like someone sat on it. Mama says we'll have to start over.

Mama sends me to the store to buy more sugar.

On my way out the door, I grab a hoop like I usually do, but

when I get outside, I remember that I'm on a mission. Miz Adeline's

party will be starting in a couple of hours. Mama has to finish the potato

salad, and we still have to make another cake.

I don't even twirl my hoop as I hurry down the street. I don't stop to blow

kisses to Miss Evelyn or wave to Mr. John in the bakery.

I'm coming out of the store when I see Jamara and Portia hoopin' on the corner of 139th and Broadway.

"We thought you weren't coming, Kameeka," says Jamara with a smirk.

I need to get the sugar back to Mama, but Jamara sounds so smug I can't stand it.

"Well, you thought wrong," I tell her.

"You ready?" she asks.

"I was born ready." And then I feel it comin' on. The itch. The Hula-Hoopin' itch.

"Whoever hoops the longest is the winner," Portia says.

As soon as she shouts "Go!" my fingers start snappin' and my feet start tappin'. My hips start swingin', and I just know I'm gonna beat Jamara today.

Neighborhood kids crowd around as Jamara and I hoop.

Cars honk and slow down. Trucks roar past, throwing up
heat and dust from the pavement.

Swish, swiggle, swish.

Jamara frowns. "You've been practicing some," she says.

"That's right, girl." A grin greater than the Brooklyn Bridge
stretches across my face.

The sun moves between the buildings, and the sidewalk
starts cooling down, but Jamara and me keep on hoopin'.

"I've got doughnuts for Miz Adeline's party," Mr. John
calls out as he closes up the bakery.

Swish, swiggle,—

"Miz Adeline's cake!" I shout.

My hoop clatters to the sidewalk. I grab it and the sugar,
and race up the block. I can hear Jamara laughing behind me.

By the time I reach our apartment, Mama is madder than a hornet. "Kameeka Hayes!" she scolds.

"I'm sorry, Mama. I saw Jamara and—"

"Girl, I don't want to hear that Hula-Hoopin' nonsense. It's too late now. Miz Adeline's already here. You take yourself on into the living room and explain to Miz Adeline why she won't have cake for her birthday."

Miz Adeline brought her own music, and she's got it turned up loud. She's sitting and listening to a jazzy blues tune, noddin' her head like a spring robin looking for a worm.

"Hi, Miz Adeline," I say. "Happy Birthday."

"Kameeka, come here, baby. Give me a kiss."

I come in close and kiss Miz Adeline's soft cheek. Then I whisper in her ear, "You don't really like cake much, do you?"

"Baby girl, you know I sure do love cake. Chocolate cake with strawberries and real whipped cream on top." She pats my arm. "Oh yes, that is my *fa-vor-ite* cake."

Miz Adeline smiles at me. I try to smile back, but my heart is racing as fast as the roller coaster at Coney Island. I can't tell her about the cake just yet.

Pretty soon the neighbors start arriving. Miss Evelyn's wearing her Sunday church hat, and Mr. John's all spruced up in a pin-striped suit. Jamara and Portia sashay in with their parents. They're still carrying their hoops from earlier today.

"Girls, I don't want to see any hoops," says Mama firmly to Jamara and Portia.

"Okay, Mrs. Hayes," says Jamara. She flashes her big, smirking smile at me. "Kameeka, you're about done with hoopin' after today, aren't you?"

I smile right back at her. "Don't you bet on it, Jamara."

Most of the presents are still unopened when Miz Adeline says, "Well, I do believe it's time for birthday cake."

I swallow hard.

"Miz Adeline," I say slowly. "We made a cake, but it didn't turn out right. Then we needed more sugar to make another one, but I didn't get the sugar back to Mama in time 'cause I was hoopin'. I was trying to beat Jamara so I could be the Hula-Hoopin' Queen of 139th Street. It's my fault there isn't any cake."

"No cake?" says Miz Adeline, raising her eyebrows.

I look over at Jamara. She's spinning one of Mr. John's doughnuts round and round on her finger like it's a Hula-Hoop.

Suddenly that gives me an idea. "I'll be right back," I yell as I race from the room.

In the kitchen I set a chocolate doughnut on a pretty plate. I add whipped cream and strawberries. Mama comes in to help. I put a candle on top, and she lights it.

As I carry the doughnut cake to Miz Adeline, Mama starts singing "Happy Birthday," and everyone joins in. The candle glows as bright as the smile on Miz Adeline's face.

"Why, this is just about perfect," Miz Adeline says, taking a bite of her doughnut birthday cake. "Now, Kameeka, did you say you were hoopin'? When I was a girl, I was the best Hula-Hooper on this block.

"Adeline, don't you start that nonsense," Miss Evelyn says as she marches on over to us. "You know very well I was the best."

Miz Adeline looks at me. "Baby girl, why don't you bring some hoops on in here and let me show this old girl what she forgot."

My eyes find Mama's. She shakes her head. But Miz Adeline's already pushing back chairs to make room. Then she slips a hoop over her head. And right then I know.

Miz Adeline's just like me. She's got the itch. The Hula-Hoopin' itch. Her fingers start snappin', and her feet start tappin'. Her hips start swingin', and before we know it that hoop is swishin' right around Miz Adeline's waist. Then she's got it swingin' around her neck.

I glance over at Mama and see a smile pulling at her lips in spite of herself. Miz Adeline shimmies the hoop down past her knees. She spins it around her ankle as she hops on one foot, then the other. With the hoop still swishin' round and round, Miz Adeline heads for the door.

Miss Evelyn grabs one of my hoops, and Mr. John grabs another. Even Mama's hips are swingin' as the whole party spills out on to the street. Everyone's got the itch. The Hula-Hoopin' itch. Pretty soon hoops are swishin' and swingin' all the way down the block.

"Kameeka, this is the best birthday party I've ever had!" Miz Adeline hollers.

Jamara hoops on over to me. "Kameeka," she says. "I know who the real Hula-Hoopin' Queen of 139th Street is."

"I do too," I say.

Jamara settles her hoop around her waist. "You ready, Kameeka?"

"I was born ready," I say.

The sidewalk is cooler than a spring rain, and the streetlights shine like stars.

Swish, swiggle, swish . . .